Astrid Lindgren

Lotta's Bike

Pictures by Ilon Wikland

R&S
BOOKS

Stockholm   New York   London   Adelaide

"I *can* ride a bike!" cried Lotta.
"I know I can — secretly."
Lotta was sitting on the gatepost outside the yellow house where she lived. She was watching Jonas and Maria racing down the hill like lightning on their bicycles. No wonder Lotta was angry. But she was not quite five, and really couldn't ride a bicycle yet — not even secretly.

"No, you're too little," said Jonas later, when they were sitting in the kitchen eating dinner.

"Besides, you haven't got a bike," said Maria, "only an old tricycle."

Lotta became even angrier. "You see," she said to Mom and Dad, "naturally, I can't ride a bike if I haven't got one." Then she nibbled at a slice of bread, whispering. "But I know I can ride a bike — secretly." There were lots of things Lotta could do secretly.

At least, she always said so. "I go to school, too," she would say, "secretly."

One time when she went to see Mrs. Berg next door, Mrs. Berg said: "How funny. Jonas and Maria have blue eyes, but Lotta's are almost green."

Then Lotta said, very firmly: "I have blue eyes, too — secretly."

Lotta always wanted to be exactly like Jonas and Maria.

"That old tricycle is no good," said Lotta that night when she got into bed with Teddy, who always slept with her. Teddy was not a bear, as you might think. He was a pig that Mom had made for Lotta. Lotta called him Teddy, and she told him everything.

"You're the only one who listens properly," she said. "Jonas and Maria never listen. And they don't understand anything, either."

Teddy was much better. He lay there quietly listening to Lotta's awful plan. "If I don't get a real bicycle on my birthday, I'll steal one," said Lotta, "secretly!"

Exactly two days later it was Lotta's birthday. She was five.
Mom and Dad and Jonas and Maria came into her room to wake her up and sang: "Happy birthday to you!" and gave her lots of presents. She got three small cars, a picture book, a jump rope, a new swing to put in the garden, and a shiny red handbag — but no bicycle.

"You can manage with the tricycle a little longer," said Dad.
Lotta liked all her presents and didn't think very much about the bicycle just then. She was happy all morning and played with her cars and looked at her picture book and jumped rope and swung on her swing.

She took a little walk with her bag on her shoulder. In the street she met the chimney sweep, who had just cleaned Mrs. Berg's chimney.

"I think red bags are nice, don't you," she said to him. The chimney sweep thought so, too, and that made Lotta even happier.

When Lotta got home and saw the tricycle standing in the corner, she kicked it.
"I can't manage with you at all," she said. She had completely forgotten how happy she was when she got the tricycle on her birthday two years before. Now she wanted a proper bicycle.
"And I know where I can steal one, too," she said.
There was an old bicycle in Mrs. Berg's shed. She had seen it there.
"I'm going to take it," she said to Teddy, "and you have to come along."

Lotta didn't want to be stealing alone. "We'll wait until Mrs. Berg is taking her afternoon nap, so she won't see us," said Lotta. What a hardened child she was!

After lunch, Lotta went to see if Mrs.
Berg had gone to sleep yet. She hadn't.
She was knitting and didn't look at all
sleepy. Scotty, Mrs. Berg's bad-tempered
little dog, rushed up, barking. Lotta was
used to that, so she wasn't afraid. "Go
ahead," she said. "Bark, even if it is my
birthday." To Mrs. Berg she said: "As I
was saying, guess whose birthday it is
today."
"Yours, of course," said Mrs. Berg. And
she went to her chest of drawers and took
out a little package. "Happy birthday,
little Lotta!" said Mrs. Berg.
Lotta ripped the package open at once.
There was a box in it, and in the box
there was a small bracelet with red and
blue and green stones. Lotta felt happy
all over. It was a beautiful bracelet. She
thanked Mrs. Berg again and again.
"You're the nicest person in the whole
world," she said, and put on the bracelet.
The stones shone in the light. "They're
just like diamonds, aren't they," she said
with satisfaction.

But then Lotta remembered her plan.
She patted Mrs. Berg's cheek and said:
"If I were you, I'd take a nap now."
"Yes, I think I will, little Lotta," said
Mrs. Berg.
And off went Lotta with her bracelet on
her wrist and Teddy in her arms.
"You see?" said Lotta. "Wasn't that
clever? Now she'll go to sleep."

Lotta sneaked into the shed and sat
down to wait. She waited and waited and
almost fell asleep herself.
At last she said: "Come on, we'll get
started."

But Lotta was small, and the bicycle was large and clumsy. It fell over four times before she got it out of the shed. It was a very awkward bicycle, thought Lotta. It scratched her legs and bumped her and kept falling over.

"Just wait until I get on," said Lotta, angrily. She said this to the bicycle. Teddy was on the back.

"Hold on," she said. "Now I'm going to ride down the hill just like Jonas and Maria." And Lotta pulled the bicycle up the steep street.

"You have to climb up before you can race down," she said breathlessly.

It's not easy to climb on the pedals of a large bicycle when you are small. But Lotta was lucky. Someone had left a box at the top of the hill, and it was just the right size for Lotta to climb on to mount the bicycle.

"Off we go, Teddy," said Lotta. And before she could finish speaking, they were racing down the hill, faster than Jonas and Maria had ever gone. Nothing like it had been seen on the street before. "Brakes!" cried Lotta. "Brakes!" But the bicycle couldn't brake and neither could she. Down the hill went Lotta, the bicycle, and Teddy, the wind whistling around them.

"Help!" Lotta shouted. "Help, help!" But the bicycle went on and on, right to the bottom of the hill, and there it crashed through the hedge in front of Mrs. Berg's house. Poor Lotta flew over the handlebars and landed headfirst in one of Mrs. Berg's rosebushes.

Then Lotta screamed so loud that Mrs. Berg woke up and stuck her head out of the window.

"What on earth," she said, "what on earth are you doing, Lotta?"

"Riding a bike," screamed Lotta. "And on my birthday, too," she cried, for she thought it was terrible to have to stand on her head in a bush on her birthday, of all days.

"Dear me," said Mrs. Berg, "where does it hurt most?"

Lotta was silent while she thought about it.

"Everywhere," she said, sullenly. "My forehead," she said.

There was a big bump on her forehead. She took a deep breath to start screaming again when she saw something even worse. She was bleeding from a scratch on her leg.

"Blood!" cried Lotta, so that she could be heard all along the street. "There's blood, on my birthday!"

And she screamed and screamed and screamed, because of the blood and the bump on her forehead, and perhaps a little bit because she had stolen the bicycle, and wondered what Mrs. Berg would say.

Mrs. Berg didn't say anything.
She just took Lotta into the kitchen,
cleaned her cuts, and put bandages on
them. Then she put the bicycle back into
the shed. She looked a little stern, Lotta
noticed.
"But I didn't steal it for long," said Lotta.
"Only while you were taking a nap. Will
you forgive me?"
"Oh, yes," said Mrs. Berg.
"But such a big bicycle is dangerous. You
should have a smaller one."
"You mean a tricycle," said Lotta,
sulking. "That's what Dad thinks."
"No, a small, real bicycle," said Mrs.
Berg.

"I wish you'd tell Dad that," said Lotta.
But then she began howling again.
"My bracelet," she screamed, "I've lost
my bracelet!"
And she really had. It was no longer
glittering on her arm.
"We'll look for it," said Mrs. Berg. They
searched and searched — in the shed, in
the street, everywhere. But they couldn't
find it.

Then Lotta went home. She wept and
screamed the whole way, so Jonas and
Maria heard her from far away as they
rode home. They met Lotta at the gate.
"Why are you crying?" asked Jonas.
"Because this is such a bad birthday,"
cried Lotta.
She told them about the bicycle and the
bracelet she had lost.
"It served you right — losing the
bracelet," said Jonas.
"Yes," said Maria. "Mrs. Berg is kind
and gives you a bracelet, and you go
straight to her shed and steal her bicycle.
It serves you right."

Lotta was silent; she felt ashamed of
herself.
"I won't talk to you," she said. And she
climbed up and sat on the top of the
gatepost to wait for Dad, who would soon
be home from work.
"I still think it's a terrible birthday," she
said to Teddy.

And there they both sat, watching Jonas and Maria riding up and down the hill as usual.

"We did that, too, didn't we," said Lotta to Teddy. But she felt sad. Jonas was riding without using his hands at all. "Mom says you're not allowed to ride like that!" said Lotta. "It's forbidden."

Just then she saw Dad coming down the street. She almost fell off the post, *because he was pulling a bicycle!* A small one, just exactly the right size for Lotta. "Now I don't understand anything," said Lotta. But she shouted, so that Mom looked out the window, and she didn't understand either.

"What's this?" said Mom. "Didn't we decide that Lotta would have to wait until next year for a bicycle?"

"Yes, I know," said Dad, "but I got this secondhand, and very cheap. She can learn to ride on it."

And although it was old and secondhand, Lotta was more pleased with the bicycle than with anything else she got on her birthday.

Jonas said: "That's not a bad bike at all! Come on, Lotta, try it!"

So Lotta tried it. Jonas ran behind to hold her on, because no one thought she could ride.

But when Jonas let go, Lotta rode by herself!

"Look, she really can ride a bike," said Mom from the window.

"Of course I can," cried Lotta.

"Look, Mrs. Berg," she called when she passed Mrs. Berg's house. "Look, I can ride a bike!"

And Mrs. Berg looked over the hedge in surprise. But then she held up her hand and said: "Look what I found hanging in the rosebush!"

She was holding Lotta's bracelet. Lotta fell off her bike in surprise; you can't ride and look at a bracelet at the same time. She didn't hurt herself, though, because she had such a small bicycle.

Jonas and Maria came to look at Lotta's bracelet, and Maria said it was the nicest bracelet she had ever seen.
"Now you don't think it's a bad birthday," said Jonas.
"I never thought it was!" said Lotta.

She rode around and around the yellow house on her secondhand bicycle, with her bracelet glittering on her arm and Teddy on the back.

Jonas and Maria rode, too. Jonas let go of the handlebars, and Lotta decided to do the same.

"Hold on," she cried to Teddy, and let go. "Look, no hands!"

Then she fell off the bike, right in the middle of the street, and although it was a small bike, she hurt her elbow quite a lot.

"You see," she said angrily to Jonas, "it *is* forbidden."

"You're just too little," said Jonas.

But Lotta just sat there rubbing her elbow, muttering softly so that only Teddy could hear her: "I *can* ride exactly like Jonas — secretly!"

Later they all went in and ate a delicious
birthday dinner.

Rabén & Sjögren Stockholm

English translation copyright © 1973 by Methuen Children's Books Ltd, London
All rights reserved
Illustrations copyright © 1971 by Ilon Wikland
Originally published in Sweden by Rabén & Sjögren
under the title *Visst kan Lotta cykla,*
text copyright © 1971 by Astrid Lindgren
Library of Congress catalog card number: 89-3772

Printed in Denmark, 1989
First American edition, 1989

ISBN 91 29 59600 9

R & S Books are distributed in the United States of Ame
by Farrar, Straus and Giroux, New York;
in the United Kingdom by Ragged Bears, Andover;
and in Australia by ERA Publications, Adelaide